Snow White
and the Seven Dwarfs

retold & illustrated by

Laura Ljungkvist

Harry N. Abrams, Inc., Publishers

Once upon a time, on a dark and wintry evening, a child was born to the king and queen. The princess was the most beautiful baby girl ever seen. Her hair was as black as the sky that night and her skin was as white as the snow that fell to the ground. She was given the name Snow White.

Snow White, so sweet and gentle, was loved and adored by everyone who met her, people and animals alike. Her parents loved her most of all. However, not long after she was born, her mother, the queen, fell ill and died.

The king then took a second wife.

The new queen was a beautiful but vain and evil woman. She could not bear the thought that anyone could be more beautiful than she.

The queen had a magic mirror into which she would gaze and ask, "Mirror, mirror, in my hand, who is the fairest in the land?" The mirror would reply, "You are fair, that is true. No one is more beautiful than you."

The seasons passed and Snow White grew into a precious little girl and then a lovely young lady. Her stepmother hardly noticed her. Until there came the day the queen asked, "Mirror, mirror, in my hand, who is the fairest in the land?" And she received a different response: "You are fair, that is true, but Snow White is more beautiful than you."

The queen's face turned green with envy and rage. She knew she had to rid the kingdom of Snow White.

The queen ordered her personal guard in the castle to take Snow White into the forest and leave her for the wild animals. So on a night as dark and cold as the one on which the princess was born, the guard took her deep into the forest and left her to be eaten by the savage beasts. However, the guard did not know how beloved Snow White was. Even the animals in the forest had heard about the sweet young princess and would not harm her.

Instead, the animals took Snow White even deeper into the forest to a tiny cottage. There she surely would be safe from the evil queen. Snow White knocked on the door. When there was no answer, and because she was so cold, the princess opened it and went inside to get warm.

A small fire burned in the fireplace and the dining table was set for dinner. There were seven tiny plates, seven tiny knives and forks, and seven tiny glasses. As a matter of fact, as Snow White looked around the cottage, she discovered seven of nearly everything. The princess sat down on the hearth in front of the fire to wait for the owners to return. But she was so tired that she soon fell asleep.

When Snow White awoke, there were seven dwarfs gathered about her. They had returned home after a long day of hard work in the mines and were very surprised to find a beautiful young princess sleeping on the floor of their cottage.

After listening to Snow White's sad story, the dwarfs took pity on her and voted to let her stay in exchange for helping around the house. Every day after the dwarfs left for work, Snow White cooked and cleaned. She sewed and knitted. Her favorite chore was working in the garden.

Before long, the queen learned from her mirror that Snow White still lived and was even more beautiful than ever. The evil woman searched the forest and soon discovered the princess working in the dwarf's garden. Stealing an apple from a tree, the queen put a deadly plan into action.

Early the next morning, after the dwarfs had gone to work in the mines, the queen slipped into the cottage. She placed the apple—now poisoned—on Snow White's breakfast plate. When the princess awoke she was delighted to find the apple, thinking it was a gift from the dwarfs. Snow White took a big bite, and before she could even swallow, she fell to the floor.

When the dwarfs returned from the mines that evening, they found Snow White's lifeless body on the floor. They were overcome with grief. Days passed, and they could not bear the thought of putting her body in the cold ground. Instead the dwarfs found a clearing in the forest where they laid Snow White to rest on a bed of roses from the garden she had so lovingly tended.

There Snow White's animal friends could
watch over her.

One day while hunting in the woods, a prince came upon Snow White lying on her bed of roses. He was the most handsome young prince in all the kingdom. His skin was the hue of the blue sky on the morning he was born, and his hair the color of the sun. He was given the name Sunray.

Thinking Snow White slept, Sunray gently shook her for he wanted to learn who she was. Doing so caused the poisoned piece of apple to fall from her mouth. In that moment, Snow White opened her eyes.

Sunray asked Snow White for her hand in marriage. When the evil queen heard of their upcoming wedding, she became so enraged she ran into the forest to find and stop them. All she found however were the wild beasts, and she was never seen or heard from again.

The wedding was celebrated with great splendor, and the seven dwarfs were the guests of honor. They all lived happily ever after.

❀ Author's Note ❀

I grew up in Gothenburg, Sweden. As we had only two television stations, there was very little children's programming and no cartoons, except on Christmas Eve. On that day at 3:00 p.m., the entire country would settle in front of their televisions for an hour of animated shows. There was always the clip from Disney's *Snow White* where the princess dances with the dwarfs (my favorite scene!). This memory I have kept alive through the years and was part of the inspiration for choosing to illustrate this classic tale. Another reason I wanted to do so was to create a more modern look for the story—one that my own daughter will relate to as well as my friends and their children.

Recreating a classic fairy tale, trying to be true to the story—visually as well as textually—yet make it my own, was both challenging and inspiring. I read a number of versions that I found on-line and in books. The original story is very long, so I chose to keep only those elements that were crucial to the plot. I wanted the story to be as simple and "clean" as the artwork so the two would work cohesively.

The artwork is gouache on watercolor paper. People often ask me why I don't create art digitally, as my work is very graphic. It might be *easier* to create on the computer, but I would lose the imperfections in my art that give it life.

The completion of this book marks the beginning of a road lined with challenges and miracles. Paul and Violet, this one's for you. I love you very much.

Designer: Becky Terhune
Production director: Hope Koturo

Library of Congress Cataloging-in-Publication Data

Ljungkvist, Laura.
Snow White / retold by Laura Ljungkvist.
p. cm.
Summary: A princess takes refuge from her wicked stepmother in the cottage of seven dwarfs.
ISBN 0-8109-4241-0
[1. Fairy tales. 2. Folklore—Germany.]
I. Snow White and the seven dwarfs. English. II. Title.

PZ8.L76 Sn 2003
398.2'0943'02—dc21

2002011923

Copyright © 2003 Laura Ljungkvist

Published in 2003 by Harry N. Abrams, Incorporated, New York. All rights reserved. No part of the contents of this book may be reproduced without the written permission of the publisher.

Printed and bound in China
10 9 8 7 6 5 4 3 2 1

Harry N. Abrams, Inc.
100 Fifth Avenue
New York, NY 10011
www.abramsbooks.com

Abrams is a subsidiary of 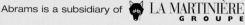 LA MARTINIÈRE
G R O U P E